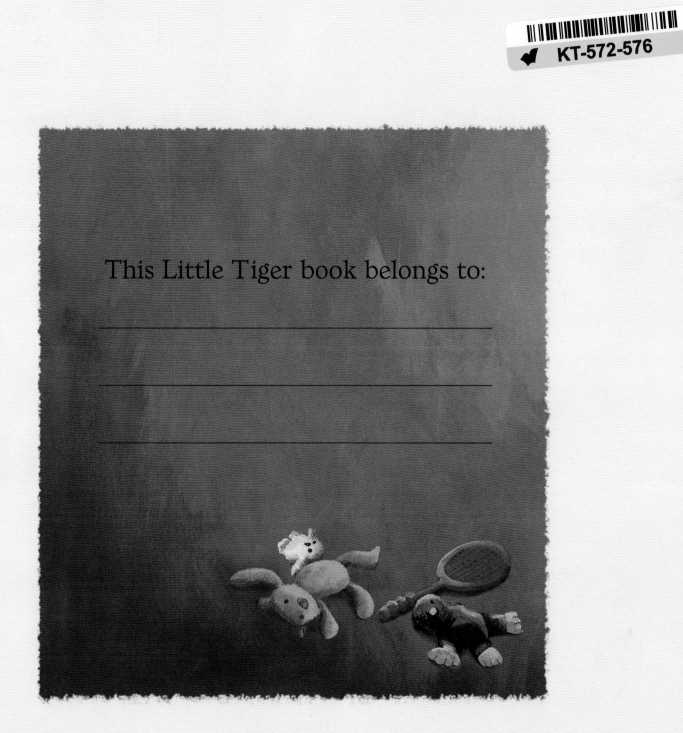

This Little Tiger book belongs to:

_____

_____

_____

For Matthew, Liz, William, Daniel and Harriet (and White Rabbit) ~ J C

For Martin and Nicola, with love ~ P B

LITTLE TIGER PRESS
1 The Coda Centre, 189 Munster Road, London SW6 6AW
www.littletiger.co.uk
First published in Great Britain 2008
This edition published 2009
Text copyright © Paul Bright 2008 • Illustrations copyright © Jane Chapman 2008
Visit Jane Chapman at www.ChapmanandWarnes.com
Paul Bright and Jane Chapman have asserted their rights to be identified as the
author and illustrator of this work under the Copyright, Designs and Patents Act, 1988
A CIP catalogue record for this book is available from the British Library
All rights reserved • ISBN 978-1-84506-764-9
Printed in China • LTP/1900/0883/0314
4 6 8 10 9 7 5

The Bears in the Bed and the Great Big Storm

Paul Bright   Jane Chapman

LITTLE TIGER PRESS

London

How the wind blew!

It howled in the treetops, so that the branches bent and creaked and the leaves shivered and shook. It blew over the hills and the high places, howling and wailing through the rocky passes.

Bear and Mrs Bear slept warm and snug and untroubled in their bed.

Then Bear felt a tugging at his
blanket. He opened one eye.
There was Baby Bear.

"There's a monster outside! I can hear
it howling and wailing and I'm scared.
Can I sleep in your bed?"
"There's no such thing as monsters,"
said Bear. "What a scaredy-bear you are."
But he pulled back the cover and
Baby Bear snuggled up, warm and safe.

How the thunder crashed!

It boomed and crackled so the house
shuddered and the windows rattled.
It grumbled and rumbled and echoed
and faded, only to boom and crash again.

Mrs Bear and Baby Bear slept warm
and snug and untroubled in their bed.
But Bear lay awake, with his paws
over his ears.

Then Bear felt a tapping on his shoulder. There was Little Bear. "There's a monster outside! Its tummy is rumbling and grumbling like it's going to eat me! Can I sleep with you?"

"There's no such thing as monsters," said Bear. "You're another scaredy-bear." But he lifted the cover and Little Bear snuggled up, warm and safe.

How the lightning flashed!

It forked and flickered, lighting the scurrying clouds and splashing quick, black shadows on the windows and the walls.

Mrs Bear and Baby Bear and Little Bear slept warm and snug and untroubled in their bed.

But Bear lay awake, with his pillow wrapped around his head.

Then Bear felt a tap on his nose. It was Young Bear.

"There's a monster outside! It has huge, twisted horns and it's making shadows on my wall. Can I come and sleep in your bed?"

"There's no such thing as monsters!" cried Bear.
But he let Young Bear climb into the bed, where he snuggled up, warm and safe.

Now Bear was wide awake.

He listened to the wind howling and the thunder crashing. He watched the lightning fork and flash.

"Young Bear's right," he thought. "The shadows on the wall *do* look like monster horns." And he pulled up the bed covers right over his head.

Suddenly, there was a

RAT-TAT-TAT at the door . . .

Everybody woke at once.

"Wh-wh-who can that be?" said Bear.

"It's probably nothing at all," said Mrs Bear.

"Go and see." And she gave Bear a little push.

Bear climbed nervously out of bed.
He picked up a candle to light his way,
and padded slowly, ever so slowly,
to the door.
  "You're all such scaredy-bears!"
he said to the others. "There's no such
thing as m-m-m-monsters!"

As he turned the
handle, the wind
blew the door open.
The candle went out.
And everything was
black as black.

Then the lightning flashed . . . .

"A MONSTER!" shouted Bear.
He jumped back in fright and dived
straight under the bed.

"It's not a monster, it's a moose!"
said Moose, stepping through the
doorway. "The storm has
blown my house away.
Can I sleep in yours?"

Bear peered out from under the bed.

   Baby Bear and Little Bear and Young Bear
laughed and laughed and laughed.

   "What a scaredy-bear you are!" they said.

"Don't you know . . .

THERE'S NO SUCH THING AS MONSTERS!"

Check out these MONSTER books from Little Tiger Press!

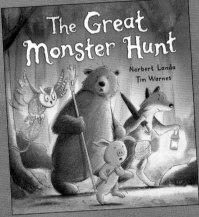

The Great Monster Hunt

Norbert Landa
Tim Warnes

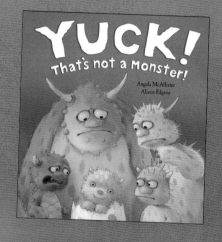

YUCK!
That's not a monster!

Angela McAllister
Alison Edgson

Who's Afraid of the Big Bad Bunny?

Steve Smallman • Caroline Pedler

There's No Such Thing As MONSTERS!

Steve Smallman • Caroline Pedler

The Not-So Scary Snorklum

Paul Bright • Anne Chapman

WHAT'S MORE SCARY THAN A SHARK?

Paul Bright • Michael Terry

For information regarding any of the above titles
or for our catalogue, please contact us:
Little Tiger Press, 1 The Coda Centre,
189 Munster Road, London SW6 6AW
Tel: 020 7385 6333 • Fax: 020 7385 7333
E-mail: contact@littletiger.co.uk
www.littletiger.co.uk